Unseen—Unfeared & Others by Francis Stevens

A pseudonym of Gertrude Barrows Bennett

Gertrude Barrows Bennett was born in Minneapolis on 18th September 1884.

She completed school up to the eighth grade, then switched to night school to study illustration, unfortunately she was never able to achieve a career in this. As a fall-back she began working as a stenographer, a career which she would keep to for the rest of her life.

But Gertrude had talent, writer's talent. Her first short story was written when she was 17. Not you would think the usual subjects of curious teenage girls with headstrong ambitions but a science fiction story entitled 'The Curious Experience of Thomas Dunbar'. She mailed the finished story to Argosy, one of the most well known of the pulp magazines. The story was published in the March 1904 issue.

Whilst her career was to be short and not at all prolific she is best remembered for her excellent ideas, many of which were way ahead of their time. By the time of her death in 1948 her pseudonym of 'Francis Stevens' could lay claim to being a respected and much admired author of science fiction and dark fantasy short stories and novels.

Index of Contents

UNSEEN

I

I had been dining with my ever-interesting friend, Mark Jenkins, at a little Italian restaurant near South Street. It was a chance meeting. Jenkins is too busy, usually, to make dinner engagements. Over our highly seasoned food and sour, thin, red wine, he spoke of little odd incidents and adventures of his profession. Nothing very vital or important, of course. Jenkins is not the sort of detective who first detects and then pours the egotistical and revealing details of achievement in the ears of every acquaintance, however appreciative.

But when I spoke of something I had seen in the morning papers, he laughed. "Poor old 'Doc' Holt! Fascinating old codger, to anyone who really knows him. I've had his friendship for years—since I was first on the city force and saved a young assistant of his from jail on a false charge. And they had to drag him into the poisoning of this young sport, Ralph Peeler!"

"Why are you so sure he couldn't have been implicated?" I asked.

But Jenkins only shook his head, with a quiet smile. "I have reasons for believing otherwise," was all I could get out of him on that score, "But," he added, "the only reason he was suspected at all is the superstitious dread of these ignorant people around him. Can't see why he lives in such a place. I know for a fact he doesn't have to. Doc's got money of his own. He's an amateur chemist and dabbler in different sorts of research work, and I suspect he's been guilty of 'showing off.' Result, they all swear he has the evil eye and holds forbidden communion with invisible powers. Smoke?"

Jenkins offered me one of his invariably good cigars, which I accepted, saying thoughtfully: "A man has no right to trifle with the superstitions of ignorant people. Sooner or later, it spells trouble."

"Did in his case. They swore up and down that he sold love charms openly and poisons secretly, and that, together with his living so near to—somebody else—got him temporarily suspected. But my tongue's running away with me, as usual!"

"As usual," I retorted impatiently, "you open up with all the frankness of a Chinese diplomat."

He beamed upon me engagingly and rose from the table, with a glance at his watch. "Sorry to leave you, Blaisdell, but I have to meet Jimmy Brennan in ten minutes."

He so clearly did not invite my further company that I remained seated for a little while after his departure; then took my own way homeward. Those streets always held for me a certain fascination, particularly at night. They are so unlike the rest of the city, so foreign in appearance, with their little shabby stores, always open until late evening, their unbelievably cheap goods, displayed as much outside the shops as in them, hung on the fronts and laid out on tables by the curb and in the street itself. Tonight, however, neither people nor stores in any sense appealed to me. The mixture of Italians, Jews and a few Negroes, mostly bareheaded, unkempt and generally unhygienic in appearance, struck me as merely revolting. They were all humans, and I, too, was human. Some way I did not like the idea.

Puzzled a trifle, for I am more inclined to sympathize with poverty than accuse it, I watched the faces that I passed. Never before had I observed how bestial, how brutal were the countenances of the dwellers in this region. I actually shuddered when an old-clothes man, a gray-bearded Hebrew, brushed me as he toiled past with his barrow.

There was a sense of evil in the air, a warning of things which it is wise for a clean man to shun and keep clear of. The impression became so strong that before I had walked two squares I began to feel physically ill. Then it occurred to me that the one glass of cheap Chianti I had drunk might have something to do with the feeling. Who knew how that stuff had been manufactured, or whether the juice of the grape entered at all into its ill-flavored composition? Yet I doubted if that were the real cause of my discomfort.

By nature I am rather a sensitive, impressionable sort of chap. In some way tonight this neighborhood, with its sordid sights and smells, had struck me wrong.

My sense of impending evil was merging into actual fear. This would never do. There is only one way to deal with an imaginative temperament like mine—conquer its vagaries. If I left South Street with this nameless dread upon me, I could never pass down it again without a recurrence of the feeling. I should simply have to stay here until I got the better of it—that was all.

I paused on a corner before a shabby but brightly lighted little drug store. Its gleaming windows and the luminous green of its conventional glass show jars made the brightest spot on the block. I realized that I was tired, but hardly wanted to go in there and rest. I knew what the company would be like at its shabby, sticky soda fountain. As I stood there, my eyes fell on a long white canvas sign across from me, and its black-and-red lettering caught my attention.

SEE THE GREAT UNSEEN!

Come in! This Means You!

FREE TO ALL!

A museum of fakes, I thought, but also reflected that if it were a show of some kind I could sit down for a while, rest, and fight off this increasing obsession of nonexistent evil. That side of the street was almost deserted, and the place itself might well be nearly empty.

II

I walked over, but with every step my sense of dread increased. Dread of I knew not what. Bodiless, inexplicable horror had me as in a net, whose strands, being intangible, without reason for existence, I could by no means throw off. It was not the people now. None of them were about me. There, in the open, lighted street, with no sight nor sound of terror to assail me, I was the shivering victim of such fear as I had never known was possible. Yet still I would not yield.

Setting my teeth, and fighting with myself as with some pet animal gone mad, I forced my steps to slowness and walked along the sidewalk, seeking entrance. Just here there were no shops, but several doors reached in each case by means of a few iron-railed stone steps. I chose the one in the middle beneath the sign. In that neighborhood there are museums, shops and other commercial enterprises conducted in many shabby old residences, such as were these. Behind the glazing of the door I had chosen I could see a dim, pinkish light, but on either side the windows were quite dark.

Trying the door, I found it unlocked. As I opened it a party of Italians passed on the pavement below and I looked back at them over my shoulder. They were gayly dressed, men, women and children, laughing and chattering to one another; probably on their way to some wedding or other festivity.

In passing, one of the men glanced up at me and involuntarily I shuddered back against the door. He was a young man, handsome after the swarthy manner of his race, but never in my life had I see a face so expressive of pure, malicious cruelty, naked and unashamed. Our eyes met and his seemed to light up with a vile gleaming, as if all the wickedness of his nature had come to a focus in the look of concentrated hate he gave me.

They went by, but for some distance I could see him watching me, chin on shoulder, till he and his party were swallowed up in the crowd of marketers farther down the street.

Sick and trembling from that encounter, merely of eyes though it had been, I threw aside my partly smoked cigar and entered. Within there was a small vestibule, whose ancient tesselated floor was grimy with the passing of many feet. I could feel the grit of dirt under my shoes, and it rasped on my rawly quivering nerves. The inner door stood partly open, and going on I found myself in a bare, dirty hallway, and was greeted by the sour, musty, poverty-stricken smell common to dwellings of the very ill-to-do. Beyond there was a stairway, carpeted with ragged grass matting. A gas jet, turned low inside a very dusty pink globe, was the light I had seen from without.

Listening, the house seemed entirely silent. Surely, this was no place of public amusement of any kind whatever. More likely it was a rooming house, and I had, after all, mistaken the entrance.

To my intense relief, since coming inside, the worst agony of my unreasonable terror had passed away. If I could only get in some place where I could sit down and be quiet, probably I should be rid of it for good. Determining to try another entrance, I was about to leave the bare hallway when one of several doors along the side of it suddenly opened and a man stepped out into the hall.

"Well?" he said, looking at me keenly, but with not the least show of surprise at my presence.

"I beg your pardon," I replied. "The door was unlocked and I came in here, thinking it was the entrance to the exhibit—what do they call it? the 'Great Unseen.' The one that is mentioned on that long white sign. Can you tell me which door is the right one?"

"I can."

With that brief answer he stopped and stared at me again. He was a tall, lean man, somewhat stooped, but possessing considerable dignity of bearing. For that neighborhood, he appeared uncommonly well dressed, and his long, smooth-shaven face was noticeable because, while his complexion was dark and his eyes coal-black, above them the heavy brows and his hair were almost silvery-white. His age might have been anything over the threescore mark.

I grew tired of being stared at. "If you can and—won't, then never mind," I observed a trifle irritably, and turned to go. But his sharp exclamation halted me.

"No!" he said. "No—no! Forgive me for pausing—it was not hesitation, I assure you. To think that one—one, even, has come! All day they pass my sign up there—pass and fear to enter. But you are different. You are not of these timorous, ignorant foreign peasants. You ask me to tell you the right door? Here it is! Here!"

And he struck the panel of the door, which he had closed behind him, so that the sharp yet hollow sound of it echoed up through the silent house.

Now it may be thought that after all my senseless terror in the open street, so strange a welcome from so odd a showman would have brought the feeling back, full force. But there is an emotion stronger, to a certain point, than fear. This queer old fellow aroused my curiosity. What kind of museum could it be that he accused the passing public of fearing to enter? Nothing really terrible, surely, or it would have been closed by the police. And normally I am not an unduly timorous person. "So it's in there, is it?" I asked, coming toward him. "And I'm to be sole audience? Come, that will be an interesting experience." I was half laughing now.

"The most interesting in the world," said the old man, with a solemnity which rebuked my lightness.

With that he opened the door, passed inward and closed it again—in my very face. I stood staring at it blankly. The panels, I remember, had been originally painted white, but now the paint was flaked and blistered, gray with dirt and dirty finger marks. Suddenly it occurred to me that I had no wish to enter there. Whatever was behind it could be scarcely worth seeing, or he would not choose such a place for its exhibition. With the old man's vanishing my curiosity had cooled, but just as I again turned to leave, the door opened and this singular showman stuck his white-eyebrowed face through the aperture. He was frowning impatiently. "Come in—come in!" he snapped, and promptly withdrawing his head, once more closed the door.

"He has something there he doesn't want should get out," was the very natural conclusion which I drew. "Well, since it can hardly be anything dangerous, and he's so anxious I should see it—here goes!"

With that I turned the soiled white porcelain handle, and entered.

The room I came into was neither very large nor very brightly lighted. In no way did it resemble a museum or lecture room. On the contrary, it seemed to have been fitted up as a quite well-appointed laboratory. The floor was linoleum-covered, there were glass cases along the walls whose shelves were filled with bottles, specimen jars, graduates, and the like. A large table in one corner bore what looked like some odd sort of camera, and a larger one in the middle of the room was fitted with a long rack filled with bottles and test tubes, and was besides littered with papers, glass slides, and various paraphernalia which my ignorance failed to identify. There were several cases of books, a few plain wooden chairs, and in the corner a large iron sink with running water.

My host of the white hair and black eyes was awaiting me, standing near the larger table. He indicated one of the wooden chairs with a thin forefinger that shook a little, either from age or eagerness. "Sit down—sit down! Have no fear but that you will be interested, my friend. Have no fear at all—of anything!"

As he said it he fixed his dark eyes upon me and stared harder than ever. But the effect of his words was the opposite of their meaning. I did sit down, because my knees gave under me, but if in the outer hall I had lost my terror, it now returned twofold upon me. Out there the light had been faint, dingily roseate, indefinite. By it I had not perceived how this old man's face was a mask of living malice—of cruelty, hate and a certain masterful contempt. Now I knew the meaning of my fear, whose warning I would not heed. Now I knew that I had walked into the very trap from which my abnormal sensitiveness had striven in vain to save me.

III

Again I struggled within me, bit at my lip till I tasted blood, and presently the blind paroxysm passed. It must have been longer in going than I thought, and the old man must have all that time been speaking, for when I could once more control my attention, hear and see him, he had taken up a position near the sink, about ten feet away, and was addressing me with a sort of "platform" manner, as if I had been the large audience whose absence he had deplored.

"And so," he was saying, "I was forced to make these plates very carefully, to truly represent the characteristic hues of each separate organism. Now, in color work of every kind the film is necessarily extremely sensitive. Doubtless you are familiar in a general way with the exquisite transparencies produced by color photography of the single-plate type."

He paused, and trying to act like a normal human being, I observed: "I saw some nice landscapes done in that way last week at an illustrated lecture in Franklin Hall."

He scowled, and made an impatient gesture at me with his hand. "I can proceed better without interruptions," he said. "My pause was purely oratorical."

I meekly subsided, and he went on in his original loud, clear voice. He would have made an excellent lecturer before a much larger audience—if only his voice could have lost that eerie, ringing note. Thinking of that I must have missed some more, and when I caught it again he was saying:

"As I have indicated, the original plate is the final picture. Now, many of these organisms are extremely hard to photograph, and microphotography in color is particularly difficult. In consequence, to spoil a plate tries the patience of the photographer. They are so sensitive that the ordinary darkroom ruby lamp would instantly ruin them, and they must therefore be developed either in darkness or by a special light produced by interposing thin sheets of tissue of a particular shade of green and of yellow between lamp and plate, and even that will often cause ruinous fog. Now I, finding it hard to handle them so, made numerous experiments with a view of discovering some glass or fabric of a color which should add to the safety of the green, without robbing it of all efficiency. All proved equally useless, but intermittently I persevered—until last week."

His voice dropped to an almost confidential tone, and he leaned slightly toward me. I was cold from my neck to my feet, though my head was burning, but I tried to force an appreciative smile.

"Last week," he continued impressively, "I had a prescription filled at the corner drug store. The bottle was sent home to me wrapped in a piece of what I first took to be whitish, slightly opalescent paper. Later I decided that it was some kind of membrane. When I questioned the druggist, seeking its source, he said it was a sheet of 'paper' that was around a bundle of herbs from South America. That he had no more, and doubted if I could trace it. He had wrapped my bottle so, because he was in haste and the sheet was handy.

"I can hardly tell you what first inspired me to try that membrane in my photographic work. It was merely dull white with a faint hint of opalescence, except when held against the light. Then it became quite translucent and quite brightly prismatic. For some reason it occurred to me that this refractive effect might help in breaking up the actinic rays—the rays which affect the sensitive emulsion. So that night I inserted it behind the sheets of green and yellow tissue, next the lamp prepared my trays and chemicals laid my plate holders to hand, turned off the white light and—turned on the green!"

There was nothing in his words to inspire fear. It was a wearisomely detailed account of his struggles with photography. Yet, as he again paused impressively, I wished that he might never speak again. I was desperately, contemptibly in dread of the thing he might say next.

Suddenly, he drew himself erect, the stoop went out of his shoulders, he threw back his head and laughed. It was a hollow sound, as if he laughed into a trumpet. "I won't tell you what I saw! Why should I? Your own eyes shall bear witness. But this much I'll say, so that you may better understand—later. When our poor, faultily sensitive vision can perceive a thing, we say that it is visible. When the nerves of touch can feel it, we say that it is tangible. Yet I tell you there are beings intangible to our physical sense, yet whose presence is felt by the spirit, and invisible to our eyes merely because those organs are not attuned to the light as reflected from their bodies. But light passed through the screen, which we are about to use has a wave length novel to the scientific world, and by it you shall see with the eyes of the flesh that which has been invisible since life began. Have no fear!"

He stopped to laugh again, and his mirth was yellow-toothed—menacing.

"Have no fear!" he reiterated, and with that stretched his hand toward the wall, there came a click and we were in black, impenetrable darkness. I wanted to spring up, to seek the door by which I had entered and rush out of it, but the paralysis of unreasoning terror held me fast.

I could hear him moving about in the darkness, and a moment later a faint green glimmer sprang up in the room. Its source was over the large sink, where I suppose he developed his precious "color plates."

Every instant, as my eyes became accustomed to the dimness, I could see more clearly. Green light is peculiar. It may be far fainter than red, and at the same time far more illuminating. The old man was standing beneath it, and his face by that ghastly radiance had the exact look of a dead man's. Besides this, however, I could observe nothing appalling.

"That," continued the man, "is the simple developing light of which I have spoken—now watch, for what you are about to behold no mortal man but myself has ever seen before."

For a moment he fussed with the green lamp over the sink. It was so constructed that all the direct rays struck downward. He opened a flap at the side, for a moment there was a streak of comforting white luminance from within, then he inserted something, slid it slowly in—and closed the flap.

The thing he put in—that South American "membrane" it must have been—instead of decreasing the light increased it—amazingly. The hue was changed from green to greenish-gray, and the whole room sprang into view, a livid, ghastly chamber, filled with—overcrawled by—what?

My eyes fixed themselves, fascinated, on something that moved by the old man's feet. It writhed there on the floor like a huge, repulsive starfish, an immense, armed, legged thing, that twisted convulsively. It was smooth, as if made of rubber, was whitish-green in color; and presently raised its great round blob of a body on tottering tentacles, crept toward my host and writhed upward—yes, climbed up his legs, his body. And he stood there, erect, arms folded, and stared sternly down at the thing which climbed.

But the room—the whole room was alive with other creatures than that. Everywhere I looked they were—centipedish things, with yard-long bodies, detestable, furry spiders that lurked in shadows, and sausage-shaped translucent horrors that moved—and floated through the air. They dived—here and there between me and the light, and I could see its bright greenness through their greenish bodies.

Worse, though; far worse than these were the things with human faces. Mask-like, monstrous, huge gaping mouths and slitlike eyes—I find I cannot write of them. There was that about them which makes their memory even now intolerable.

The old man was speaking again, and every word echoed in my brain like the ringing of a gong. "Fear nothing! Among such as these do you move every hour of the day and night. Only you and I have seen, for God is merciful and has spared our race from sight. But I am not merciful! I loathe the race which gave these creatures birth—the race which might be so surrounded by invisible, unguessed but blessed beings—and chooses these for its companions! All the world shall see and know. One by one shall they come here, learn the truth, and perish. For who can survive the ultimate of terror? Then I, too, shall find peace, and leave the earth to its heritage of man-created horrors. Do you know what these are— whence they come?"

This voice boomed now like a cathedral bell. I could not answer, him, but he waited for no reply. "Out of the ether—out of the omnipresent ether from whose intangible substance the mind of God made the planets, all living things, and man—man has made these! By his evil thoughts, by his selfish panics, by his lusts and his interminable, never-ending hate he has made them, and they are everywhere! Fear nothing—but see where there comes to you, its creator, the shape and the body of your FEAR!"

And as he said it I perceived a great Thing coming toward me—a Thing—but consciousness could endure no more. The ringing, threatening voice merged in a roar within my ears, there came a merciful dimming of the terrible, lurid vision, and blank nothingness succeeded upon horror too great for bearing.

IV

There was a dull, heavy pain above my eyes. I knew that they were closed, that I was dreaming, and that the rack full of colored bottles which I seemed to see so clearly was no more than a part of the dream. There was some vague but imperative reason why I should rouse myself. I wanted to awaken, and thought that by staring very hard indeed I could dissolve this foolish vision of blue and yellow-brown bottles. But instead of dissolving they grew clearer, more solid and substantial of appearance, until suddenly the rest of my senses rushed to the support of sight, and I became aware that my eyes were open, the bottles were quite real, and that I was sitting in a chair, fallen sideways so that my cheek rested most uncomfortably on the table which held the rack.

I straightened up slowly and with difficulty, groping in my dulled brain for some clue to my presence in this unfamiliar place, this laboratory that was lighted only by the rays of an arc light in the street outside its three large windows. Here I sat, alone, and if the aching of cramped limbs meant anything, here I had sat for more than a little time.

Then, with the painful shock which accompanies awakening to the knowledge of some great catastrophe, came memory. It was this very room, shown by the street lamp's rays to be empty of life, which I had seen thronged with creatures too loathsome for description. I staggered to my feet, staring fearfully about. There were the glass-floored cases, the bookshelves, the two tables with their burdens, and the long iron sink above which, now only a dark blotch of shadow, hung the lamp from which had emanated that livid, terrifically revealing illumination. Then the experience had been no dream, but a frightful reality. I was alone here now. With callous indifference my strange host had allowed me to remain for hours unconscious, with not the least effort to aid or revive me. Perhaps, hating me so, he had hoped that I would die there.

At first I made no effort to leave the place. Its appearance filled me with reminiscent loathing. I longed to go, but as yet felt too weak and ill for the effort. Both mentally and physically my condition was deplorable, and for the first time I realized that a shock to the mind may react upon the body as vilely as any debauch of self-indulgence.

Quivering in every nerve and muscle, dizzy with headache and nausea, I dropped back into the chair, hoping that before the old man returned I might recover sufficient self-control to escape him. I knew that he hated me, and why. As I waited, sick, miserable, I understood the man. Shuddering, I recalled the loathsome horrors he had shown me. If the mere desires and emotions of mankind were daily carnified in such forms as those, no wonder that he viewed his fellow beings with detestation and longed only to destroy them.

I thought, too, of the cruel, sensuous faces I had seen in the streets outside—seen for the first time, as if a veil had been withdrawn from eyes hitherto blinded by self-delusion. Fatuously trustful as a month-old puppy, I had lived in a grim, evil world, where goodness is a word and crude selfishness the only actuality. Drearily my thoughts drifted back through my own life, its futile purposes, mistakes and activities. All of evil that I knew returned to overwhelm me. Our gropings toward divinity were a sham, a writhing sunward of slime—covered beasts who claimed sunlight as their heritage, but in their hearts preferred the foul and easy depths.

Even now, though I could neither see nor feel them, this room, the entire world, was acrawl with the beings created by our real natures. I recalled the cringing, contemptible fear to which my spirit had so readily yielded, and the faceless Thing to which the emotion had given birth.

Then abruptly, shockingly, I remembered that every moment I was adding to the horde. Since my mind could conceive only repulsive incubi, and since while I lived I must think, feel, and so continue to shape them, was there no way to check so abominable a succession? My eyes fell on the long shelves with their many-colored bottles. In the chemistry of photography there are deadly poisons—I knew that. Now was the time to end it—now! Let him return and find his desire accomplished. One good thing I could do, if one only. I could abolish my monster-creating self.

V

My friend Mark Jenkins is an intelligent and usually a very careful man. When he took from "Smiler" Callahan a cigar which had every appearance of being excellent, innocent Havana, the act denoted both intelligence and caution. By very clever work he had traced the poisoning of young Ralph Peeler to Mr. Callahan's door, and he believed this particular cigar to be the mate of one smoked by Peeler just previous to his demise. And if, upon arresting Callahan, he had not confiscated this bit of evidence, it would have doubtless been destroyed by its regrettably unconscientious owner.

But when Jenkins shortly afterward gave me that cigar, as one of his own, he committed one of those almost inconceivable blunders which, I think, are occasionally forced upon clever men to keep them from overweening vanity. Discovering his slight mistake, my detective friend spent the night searching for his unintended victim, myself; and that his search was successful was due to Pietro Marini, a young Italian of Jenkins' acquaintance, whom he met about the hour of 2:00 A.M. returning from a dance.

Now, Marini had seen me standing on the steps of the house where Doctor Frederick Holt had his laboratory and living rooms, and he had stared at me, not with any ill intent, but because he thought I was the sickest-looking, most ghastly specimen of humanity that he had ever beheld. And, sharing the superstition of his South Street neighbors, he wondered if the worthy doctor had poisoned me as well as Peeler. This suspicion he imparted to Jenkins, who, however, had the best of reasons for believing otherwise. Moreover, as he informed Marini, Holt was dead, having drowned himself late the previous afternoon. An hour or so after our talk in the restaurant, news of his suicide reached Jenkins.

It seemed wise to search any place where a very sick-looking young man had been seen to enter, so Jenkins came straight to the laboratory. Across the fronts of those houses was the long sign with its mysterious inscription, "See the Great Unseen," not at all mysterious to the detective. He knew that next door to Doctor Holt's the second floor had been thrown together into a lecture room, where at certain hours a young man employed by settlement workers displayed upon a screen stereopticon views of various deadly bacilli, the germs of diseases appropriate to dirt and indifference. He knew, too, that Doctor Holt himself had helped the educational effort along by providing some really wonderful lantern slides, done by micro-color photography.

On the pavement outside, Jenkins found the two-thirds remnant of a cigar, which he gathered in and came up the steps, a very miserable and self-reproachful detective. Neither outer nor inner door was locked, and in the laboratory he found me, alive, but on the verge of death by another means that he had feared.

In the extreme physical depression following my awakening from drugged sleep, and knowing nothing of its cause, I believed my adventure fact in its entirety. My mentality was at too low an ebb to resist its dreadful suggestion. I was searching among Holt's various bottles when Jenkins burst in. At first I was merely annoyed at the interruption of my purpose, but before the anticlimax of his explanation the mists of obsession drifted away and left me still sick in body, but in spirit happy as any man may well be who has suffered a delusion that the world is wholly bad—and learned that its badness springs from his own poisoned brain.

The malice which I had observed in every face, including young Marini's, existed only in my drug-affected vision. Last week's "popular-science" lecture had been recalled to my subconscious mind—the mind that rules dreams and delirium—by the photographic apparatus in Holt's workroom. "See the Great Unseen" assisted materially, and even the corner drug store before which I had paused, with its green-lit show vases, had doubtless played a part. But presently, following something Jenkins told me, I was driven to one protest. "If Holt was not here," I demanded, "if Holt is dead, as you say, how do you account for the fact that I, who have never seen the man, was able to give you an accurate description which you admit to be that of Doctor Frederick Holt?"

He pointed across the room. "See that?" It was a life-size bust portrait, in crayons, the picture of a white-haired man with bushy eyebrows and the most piercing black eyes I had ever seen—until the previous evening. It hung facing the door and near the windows, and the features stood out with a strangely lifelike appearance in the white rays of the arc lamp just outside. "Upon entering," continued Jenkins, "the first thing you saw was that portrait, and from it your delirium built a living, speaking man. So, there are your white-haired showman, your unnatural fear, your color photography and your pretty green golliwogs all nicely explained for you, Blaisdell, and thank God you're alive to hear the explanation. If you had smoked the whole of that cigar—well, never mind. You didn't. And now, my very dear friend, I think it's high time that you interviewed a real, flesh-and-blood doctor. I'll phone for a taxi."

"Don't," I said. "A walk in the fresh air will do me more good than fifty doctors."

"Fresh air! There's no fresh air on South Street in July," complained Jenkins, but reluctantly yielded.

I had a reason for my preference. I wished to see people, to meet face to face even such stray prowlers as might be about at this hour, nearer sunrise than midnight, and rejoice in the goodness and kindliness of the human countenance—particularly as found in the lower classes.

But even as we were leaving there occurred to me a curious inconsistency.

"Jenkins," I said, "you claim that the reason Holt, when I first met him in the hall, appeared to twice close the door in my face, was because the door never opened until I myself unlatched it."

"Yes," confirmed Jenkins, but he frowned, foreseeing my next question.

"Then why, if it was from that picture that I built so solid, so convincing a vision of the man, did I see Holt in the hall before the door was open?"

"You confuse your memories," retorted Jenkins rather shortly.

"Do I? Holt was dead at that hour, but—I tell you I saw Holt outside the door! And what was his reason for committing suicide?"

Before my friend could reply I was across the room, fumbling in the dusk there at the electric lamp above the sink. I got the tin flap open and pulled out the sliding screen, which consisted of two sheets of glass with fabric between, dark on one side, yellow on the other. With it came the very thing I dreaded—a sheet of whitish, parchmentlike, slightly opalescent stuff.

Jenkins was beside me as I held it at arm's length toward the windows. Through it the light of the arc lamp fell—divided into the most astonishingly brilliant rainbow hues. And instead of diminishing the light, it was perceptibly increased in the oddest way. Almost one thought that the sheet itself was luminous, and yet when held in shadow it gave off no light at all.

"Shall we—put it in the lamp again—and try it?" asked Jenkins slowly, and in his voice there was no hint of mockery.

I looked him straight in the eyes. "No," I said, "we won't. I was drugged. Perhaps in that condition I received a merciless revelation of the discovery that caused Holt's suicide, but I don't believe it. Ghost or no ghost, I refuse to ever again believe in the depravity of the human race. If the air and the earth are teeming with invisible horrors, they are not of our making, and—the study of demonology is better let alone. Shall we burn this thing, or tear it up?"

"We have no right to do either," returned Jenkins thoughtfully, "but you know, Blaisdell, there's a little too darn much realism about some parts of your 'dream.' I haven't been smoking any doped cigars; but when you held that up to the light, I'll swear I saw—well, never mind. Burn it—send it back to the place it came from."

"South America?" said I.

"A hotter place than that. Burn it."

So he struck a match and we did. It was gone in one great white flash.

A large place was given by morning papers to the suicide of Doctor Frederick Holt, caused, it was surmised, by mental derangement brought about by his unjust implication in the Peeler murder. It seemed an inadequate reason, since he had never been arrested, but no other was ever discovered.

Of course, our action in destroying that "membrane" was illegal and rather precipitate, but, though he won't talk about it, I know that Jenkins agrees with me—doubt is sometimes better than certainty, and there are marvels better left unproved. Those, for instance, which concern the Powers of Evil.

Behind the Curtain

It was after nine o'clock when the bell rang, and descending to the dimly lighted hall I opened the front door, at first on the chain to be sure of my visitor. Seeing, as I had hoped, the face of our friend, Ralph Quentin, I took off the chain and he entered with a blast of sharp November air for company. I had to throw my weight upon the door to close it against the wind.

As he removed his hat and cloak he laughed good-humoredly.

"You're very cautious, Santallos. I thought you were about to demand a password before admitting me."

"It is well to be cautious," I retorted. "This house stands somewhat alone, and thieves are everywhere."

"It would require a thief of considerable muscle to make off with some of your treasures. That stone tomb-thing, for instance; what do you call it?"

"The Beni Hassan sarcophagus. Yes. But what of the gilded inner case, and what of the woman it contains? A thief of judgment and intelligence might covet that treasure and strive to deprive me of it. Don't you agree?"

He only laughed again, and counterfeited a shudder.

"The woman! Don't remind me that such a brown, shriveled, mummy-horror was ever a woman!"

"But she was. Doubtless in her day my poor Princess of Naarn was soft, appealing; a creature of red, moist lips and eyes like stars in the black Egyptian sky. 'The Songstress of the House' she was called, ere she became Ta-Nezem the Osirian. But I keep you standing here in the cold hall. Come upstairs with me. Did I tell you that Beatrice is not here tonight?"

"No?" His intonation expressed surprise and frank disappointment. "Then I can't say good-by to her? Didn't you receive my note? I'm to take Sanderson's place as manager of the sales department in Chicago, and I'm off tomorrow morning."

"Congratulations. Yes, we had your note, but Beatrice was given an opportunity to join some friends on a Southern trip. The notice was short, but of late she has not been so well and I urged her to go. This November air is cruelly damp and bitter."

"What was it-a yachting cruise?"

"A long cruise. She left this afternoon. I have been sitting in her boudoir, Quentin, thinking of her, and I'll tell you about it there-if you don't mind?"

"Wherever you like," he conceded, though in a tone of some surprise. I suppose he had not credited me with so much sentiment, or thought it odd that I should wish to share it with another, even so good a friend as he. "You must find it fearfully lonesome here without Bee," he continued.

"A trifle." We were ascending the dark stairs now. "After tonight, however, things will be quite different. Do you know that I have sold the house?"

"No! Why, you are full of astonishments, old chap. Found a better place with more space for your tear-jars and tombstones?"

He meant, I assumed, a witty reference to my collection of Coptic and Egyptian treasures, well and dearly bought, but so much trash to a man of Quentin's youth and temperament.

I opened the door of my wife's boudoir, and it was pleasant to pass into such rosy light and warmth out of the stern, dark cold of the hall. Yet it was an old house, full of unexpected drafts. Even here there was a draft so strong that a heavy velour curtain at the far side of the room continually rippled and billowed out, like a loose rose-colored sail. Never far enough, though, to show what was behind it.

My friend settled himself on the frail little chair that stood before my wife's dressing-table. It was the kind of chair that women love and most men loathe, but Quentin, for all his weight and stature, had a touch of the feminine about him, or perhaps of the feline. Like a cat, he moved delicately. He was blond and tall, with fine, regular features, a ready laugh, and the clean charm of youth about him-also its occasional blundering candor.

As I looked at him sitting there, graceful, at ease, I wished that his mind might have shared the litheness of his body. He could have understood me so much better.

"I have indeed found a place for my collections," I observed, seating myself near by. "In fact, with a single exception-the Ta-Nezem sarcophagus-the entire lot is going to the dealers." Seeing his expression of astonished disbelief I continued: "The truth is, my dear Quentin, that J have been guilty of gross injustice to our Beatrice. I have been too good a collector and too neglectful a husband. My 'tear-jars and tombstones,' in fact, have enjoyed an attention that might better have been elsewhere bestowed.

Yes, Beatrice has left me alone, but the instant that some few last affairs are settled I intend rejoining her. And you yourself are leaving. At least, none of us three will be left to miss the others' friendship."

"You are quite surprising tonight, Santallos. But, by Jove, I'm not sorry to hear any of it! It's not my place to criticize, and Bee's not the sort to complain. But living here in this lonely old barn of a house, doing all her own work, practically deserted by her friends, must have been-"

"Hard, very hard," I interrupted him softly, "for one so young and lovely as our Beatrice. But if I have been blind at least the awakening has come. You should have seen her face when she heard the news. It was wonderful. We were standing, just she and I, in the midst of my tear-jars and tombstones-my 'chamber of horrors' she named it. You are so apt at amusing phrases, both of you. We stood beside the great stone sarcophagus from the Necropolis of Beni Hassan. Across the trestles beneath it lay the gilded inner case wherein Ta-Nezem the Osirian had slept out so many centuries. You know its appearance. A thing of beautiful, gleaming lines, like the quaint, smiling image of a golden woman.

"Then I lifted the lid and showed Beatrice that the one-time songstress, the handmaiden of Amen, slept there no more, and the case was empty. You know, too, that Beatrice never liked my princess. For a jest she used to declare that she was jealous. Jealous of a woman dead and ugly so many thousand years! Or-but that was only in anger-that I had bought Ta-Nezem with what would have given her, Beatrice, all the pleasure she lacked in life. Oh, she was not too patient to reproach me, Quentin, but only in anger and hot blood.

"So I showed her the empty case, and I said, 'Beloved wife, never again need you be jealous of Ta-Nezem. All that is in this room save her and her belongings I have sold, but her I could not bear to sell. That which I love, no man else shall share or own. So I have destroyed her. I have rent her body to brown, aromatic shreds. I have burned her; it is as if she had never been. And now, dearest of the dear, you shall take for your own all the care, all the keeping that Heretofore I have lavished upon the Princess of Naam.'

"Beatrice turned from the empty case as if she could scarcely believe her hearing, but when she saw by the look in my eyes that I meant exactly what I said, neither more nor less, you should have seen her face, my dear Quentin-you should have seen her face!"

"I can imagine." He laughed, rather shortly. For some reason my guest seemed increasingly ill at ease, and glanced continually about the little rose-and-white room that was the one luxurious, thoroughly feminine corner-that and the cold, dark room behind the curtain-in what he had justly called my "barn of a house."

"Santallos," he continued abruptly, and I thought rather rudely, "you should have a portrait done as you look tonight. You might have posed for one of those stern old hidalgos of-which painter was it who did so many Spanish dons and donesses?"

"You perhaps mean Velasquez," I answered with mild courtesy, though secretly and as always his crude personalities displeased me. "My father, you may recall, was of Cordova in southern Spain. But-must you go so soon? First drink one glass with me to our missing Beatrice. See how I was warming my blood against the wind that blows in, even here. The wine is Amontillado, some that was sent me by a friend of my father's from the very vineyards where the grapes were grown and pressed. And for many years it has ripened since it came here. Before she went, Beatrice drank of it from one of these same glasses. True wine of Montilla! See how it lives-like fire in amber, with a glimmer of blood behind it."

I held high the decanter and the light gleamed through it upon his face.

"Amontillado! Isn't that a kind of sherry? I'm no connoisseur of wines, as you know. But-Amontillado."

For a moment he studied the wine I had given him, liquid flame in the crystal glass. Then his face cleared.

"I remember the association now. 'The Cask of Amontillado.' Ever read the story?"

"I seem to recall it dimly."

"Horrible, fascinating sort of a yarn. A fellow takes his trustful friend down into the cellars to sample some wine, traps him and walls him up in a niche. Buries him alive, you understand. Read it when I was a youngster, and it made a deep impression, partly, I think, because I couldn't for the life of me comprehend a nature-even an Italian nature-desiring so horrible a form of vengeance. You're half Latin yourself, Santallos. Can you elucidate?"

"I doubt if you would ever understand," I responded slowly, wondering how even Quentin could be so crude, so tactless. "Such a revenge might have its merits, since the offender would be a long time dying. But merely to kill seems to me so pitifully inadequate. Now I, if I were driven to revenge, should never be contented by killing. I should wish to follow."

"What-beyond the grave?"

I laughed. "Why not? Wouldn't that be the very apotheosis of hatred? I'm trying to interpret the Latin nature, as you asked me to do."

"Confound you, for an instant I thought you were serious. The way you said it made me actually shiver!"

"Yes," I observed, "or perhaps it was the draft. See, Quentin, how that curtain billows out."

His eyes followed my glance. Continually the heavy, rose-colored curtain that wag hung before the door of my wife's bedroom bulged outward, shook and quivered like a bellying sail, as draperies will with a wind behind them.

His eyes strayed from the curtain, met mine and fell again to the wine in his glass. Suddenly he drained it, not as would a man who was a judge of wines, but hastily, indifferently, without thought for its flavor or bouquet. I raised my glass in the toast he had forgotten.

"To our Beatrice," I said, and drained mine also, though with more appreciation.

"To Beatrice-of course." He looked at the bottom of his empty glass, then before I could offer to refill it, rose from his chair.

"I must go, old man. When you write to Bee, tell her I'm sorry to have missed her."

"Before she could receive a letter from me I shall be with her-I hope. How cold the house is tonight, and the wind breathes everywhere. See how the curtain blows, Quentin."

"So it does." He set his glass on the tray beside the decanter. Upon first entering the room he had been smiling, but now his straight, fine brows were drawn in a perpetual, troubled frown, his eyes looked here and there, and would never meet mine-which were steady. "There's a wind," he added, "that blows along this wall-curious. One can't notice any draft there, either. But it must blow there, and of course the curtain billows out."

"Yes," I said. "Of course it billows out."

"Or is there another door behind that curtain?"

His careful ignorance of what any fool might infer from mere appearance brought an involuntary smile to my lips. Nevertheless, I answered him.

"Yes, of course there is a door. An open door."

His frown deepened. My true and simple replies appeared to cause him a certain irritation.

"As I feel now," I added, "even to cross the room would be an effort. I am tired and weak tonight. As Beatrice once said, my strength beside yours is as a child's to that of a grown man. Won't you close that door for me, dear friend?"

"Why-yes, I will. I didn't know you were ill. If that's the case, you shouldn't be alone in this empty house. Shall I stay with you for a while?"

As he spoke he walked across the room. His hand was on the curtain, but before it could be drawn aside my voice checked him.

"Quentin," I said, "are even you quite strong enough to close that door?"

Looking back at me, chin on shoulder, his face appeared scarcely familiar, so drawn was it in lines of bewilderment and half-suspicion.

"What do you mean? You are very odd tonight. Is the door so heavy then? What door is it?"

I made no reply.

As if against their owner's will his eyes fled from mine, he turned and hastily pushed aside the heavy drapery.

Behind it my wife's bedroom lay dark and cold, with windows open to the invading winds.

And erect in the doorway, uncovered, stood an ancient gilded coffin-case. It was the golden casket of Ta-Nezem, but its occupant was more beautiful than the poor, shriveled Songstress of Naam.

Bound across her bosom were the strange, quaint jewels which had been found in the sarcophagus. Ta-Nezem's amulets-heads of Hathor and Horus the sacred eye, the uroeus, even the heavy dull-green scarab, the amulet for purity of heart-there they rested upon the bosom of her who had been mistress of my house, now Beatrice the Osirian. Beneath them her white, stiff body was enwrapped in the same crackling dry, brown linen bands, impregnated with the gums and resins of embalmers dead these many thousand years, which had been about the body of Ta-Nezem.

Above the white translucence of her brow appeared the winged disk, emblem of Ra. The twining golden bodies of its supporting uraeii, its cobras of Egypt, were lost in the dusk of her hair, whose soft fineness yet lived and would live so much longer than the flesh of any of us three.

Yes, I had kept my word and given to Beatrice all that had been Ta-Nezem's, even to the sarcophagus itself, for in my will it was written that she be placed in it for final burial.

Like the fool he was, Quentin stood there, staring at the unclosed, frozen eyes of my Beatrice-and his. Stood till that which had been in the wine began to make itself felt. He faced me then, but with so absurd and childish a look of surprise that, despite the courtesy due a guest, I laughed and laughed.

I, too, felt warning throes, but to me the pain was no more than a gage-a measure of his sufferings stimulus to point the phrases in which I told him all I knew and had guessed of him and Beatrice, and thus drive home the jest.

But I had never thought that a man of Quentin's youth and strength could die so easily. Beatrice, frail though she was, had taken longer to die.

He could not even cross the room to stop my laughter, but at the first step stumbled, fell, and in a very little while lay at the foot of the gilded case.

After all, he was not so strong as I. Beatrice had seen. Her still, cold eyes saw all. How he lay there, his fine, lithe body contorted, worthless for any use till its substance should have been cast again in the melting-pot of dissolution, while I who had drunk of the same draft, suffered the same pangs, yet stood and found breath for mockery.

So I poured myself another glass of that good Cordovan wine, and I raised it to both of them and drained it, laughing.

"Quentin," I cried, "you asked what door, though your thought was that you had passed that way before, and feared that I guessed your, knowledge. But there are doors and doors, dear, charming friend, and one that is heavier than any other. Close it if you can. Close it now in my face, who otherwise will follow even whither you have gone-the heavy, heavy door of the Osiris, Keeper of the House of Death!"

Thus I dreamed of doing and speaking. It was so vivid, the dream, that awakening in the darkness of my room I could scarcely believe that it had been other than reality. True, I lived, while in my dream I had shared the avenging poison. Yet my veins were still hot with the keen passion of triumph, and my eyes filled with the vision of Beatrice, dead-dead in Ta-Nezem's casket.

Unreasonably frightened. I sprang from bed, flung on a dressing-gown, and hurried out. Down the hallway I sped, swiftly and silently, at the end of it unlocked heavy doors with a tremulous hand, switched on lights, lights and more lights, till the great room of my collection was ablaze with them, and as my treasures sprang into view I sighed, like a man reaching home from a perilous journey.

The dream was a lie.

There, fronting me, stood the heavy empty sarcophagus; there on the trestles before it lay the gilded case, a thing of beautiful, gleaming lines, like the smiling image of a golden woman.

I stole across the room and softly, very softly, lifted the upper half of the beautiful lid, peering within. The dream indeed was a lie.

Happy as a comforted child I went to my room again. Across the hall the door of my wife's boudoir stood partly open.

In the room beyond a faint light was burning, and I could see the rose-colored curtain sway slightly to a draft from some open window.

Yesterday she had come to me and asked for her freedom. I had refused, knowing to whom she would turn, and hating him for his youth, and his crudeness and his secret scorn of me.

But had I done well? They were children, those two, and despite my dream I was certain that their foolish, youthful ideals had kept them from actual sin against my honor. But what if, time passing, they might change? Or, Quentin gone, my lovely Beatrice might favor another, young as he and not so scrupulous?

Every one, they say, has a streak of incipient madness. I recalled the frenzied act to which my dream jealousy had driven me. Perhaps it was a warning, the dream. What if my father's jealous blood should some day betray me, drive me to the insane destruction of her I held most dear and sacred.

I shuddered, then smiled at the swaying curtain. Beatrice was too beautiful for safety. She should have her freedom.

Let her mate with Ralph Quentin or whom she would, Ta-Nezem must rest secure in her gilded house of death. My brown, perfect, shriveled Princess of the Nile! Destroyed-rent to brown, aromatic shreds-burned-destroyed-and her beautiful coffin-case desecrated as I had seen it in my vision'.

Again I shuddered, smiled and shook my head sadly at the swaying, rosy curtain.

"You are too lovely, Beatrice," I said, "and my father was a Spaniard. You shall have your freedom!"

I entered my room and lay down to sleep again, at peace and content.

The dream, thank God, was a lie.

In this our well-advertised, modern world, crammed with engines, death-dealing shells, life-dealing serums, and science, he who listens to "old wives' tales" is counted idle. He who believes them, a superstitious fool. Yet there are some legends which have a strange, deathless habit of recrudescence in many languages and lands.

Of one such I have a story to tell. It was related to me by a well-known specialist in nervous diseases, not as an instance of the possible truth behind fable, but as a curious case in which—I quote his words— "the delusions of a diseased brain were reflected by a second and otherwise sound mentality."

No doubt his view was the right one. And yet, at the finish, I had the strangest flash of feeling. As if, somewhere, some time, I, like young Wharton, had stood and seen against blue sky—Elva, of the sky-hued scarf and the yellow honeysuckles.

But my part is neither to feel nor surmise. I will tell the story as I heard it, save for substitution of fictitious names for the real ones. My quotations from the red notebook are verbatim.

Theron Tademus, A.A.S., F.E.S., D.S., et cetera, occupied the chair of biology in a not-unfamed university. He was the author of a treatise on cytology, since widely used as a textbook, and of several important brochures on the more obscure infusoria. As a boy he had been—in appearance—a romantically charming person. The age of thirty-seven found him still handsome in a cold, fine-drawn manner, but almost inhumanly detached from any save scientific interests.

Then, at the height of his career, he died. Having entered his class-room with intent to deliver the first lecture of the fall term, he walked to his desk, laid down a small, red note-book, turned, opened his mouth, went ghastly white and subsided. His assistant, young Wharton, was first to reach him and first to discover the shocking truth.

Tademus was unmarried, and his will bequeathed all he possessed to the university.

The little red book was not at first regarded as important. Supposed to contain notes for his lecture, it was laid aside. On being at last read, however, by his assistant in course of arranging his papers, the book was found to contain not notes, but a diary covering the summer just passed.

Barring the circumstances of one peculiar incident, Wharton already knew the main facts of that summer.

Tademus, at the insistence of his physician—the specialist aforesaid—had spent July and August in the Carolina Mountains not far north from the famous resort, Asheville. Dr. Locke was friend as well as medical adviser, and he lent his patient the use of a bungalow he owned there.

It was situated in a beautiful, but lonely spot, to which the nearest settlement was Carcassonne. In the valley below stood a tiny railroad station, but Carcassonne was not built up around this, nor was it a town at all in the ordinary sense.

A certain landscape painter had once raised him a house on that mountainside, at a place chosen for its magnificent view. Later, he was wont to invite thither, for summer sketching, one or two of his more favored pupils. Later still, he increased this number. For their accommodation other structures were raised near his mountain studio, and the Blue Ridge summer class became an established fact, with a name of its own and a rather large membership.

Two roads led thither from the valley. One, that most in use by the artist colonists, was as good and broad as any Carolina mountain road could hope to be. The other, a winding, narrow, yellow track, passed the lonely bungalow of Dr. Locke, and at last split into two paths, one of which led on to further heights, the second to Carcassonne.

The distance between colony and bungalow was considerable, and neither was visible to the other. Tademus was not interested in art, and, as disclosed by the red book, he was not even aware of Carcassonne's existence until some days after his arrival at the bungalow.

Solitude, long walks, deep breathing, and abstinence from work or sustained thought had been Dr. Locke's prescription, accepted with seeming meekness by Tademus.

Nevertheless, but a short time passed till Wharton received a telegram from the professor ordering him to pack and send by express certain apparatus, including a microscope and dissecting stand. The assistant obeyed.

Another fortnight and Dr. Locke in turn received an urgent wire. It was from Jake Higgins, the Negro caretaker whom he had "lent" to Tademus along with the bungalow.

Leaving his practice to another man's care, Dr. Locke fled for the Carolina Blue Ridge.

He found his caretaker and his bungalow, but no Tademus.

By Jake's story, the professor had gone to walk one afternoon and had not returned. Having wired Locke, the caretaker had otherwise done his best. He notified the county sheriff, and search parties scoured the mountains. At his appeal, too, the entire Carcassonnian colony, male and female, turned out with enthusiasm to hunt for Tademus. Many of them carried easel and sketch-box along, and for such it is to be feared that their humane search ended with the discovery of any tempting "tit" in the scenic line.

However, the colony's efforts were at least as successful as the sheriff's or indeed those of anyone else.

Shortly before Tademus' vanishment, a band of gypsies had settled themselves in a group of old, empty, half-ruined shacks, about a mile from Locke's bungalow.

Suspicion fell upon them. A posse visited the encampment, searched it and questioned every member of the migrant band. They were a peculiarly ill-favored set, dirty and villainous of feature. Nothing, however, could be found of either the missing professor or anything belonging to him.

The posse left, after a quarrel that came near to actual fighting. A dog—a wretched, starved yellow cur—had attacked one of the deputies and set its teeth in his boot. He promptly shot it. In their resentment, the dog's owners drew knives.

The posse were more efficiently armed, and under threat of the latter's rifles and shotguns, the gypsies reconsidered. They were warned to pack up and leave, and following a few days' delay, they obeyed the mandate.

On the very morning of their departure, which was also the eighth day after Tademus' disappearance, Dr. Locke sat down gloomily to breakfast. The search, he thought, must be further extended. Let it cover the whole Blue Ridge, if need be. Somewhere in those mountains was a friend and patient whom he did not propose to lose.

At one side of the breakfast room was a door. It led into the cleared-out bedroom which Locke had, with indignation, discovered to have been converted into a laboratory by the patient he had sent here to "rest."

Suddenly this door opened. Out walked Theron Tademus.

He seemed greatly amazed to find Locke there, and said that he had come in shortly after midnight and been in his laboratory ever since.

Questioned as to his whereabouts before that, he replied surprisingly that throughout the week he had been visiting with friends in Carcassonne.

Dr. Locke doubted his statement. And reasonably.

Artists are not necessarily liars, and every artist and near-artist in the Carcassonne colony had not only denied knowledge of the professor, but spent a good part of the week helping hunt for him.

Later, after insisting that Locke accompany him to Carcassonne and meet his friends there, Tademus suddenly admitted that he had not previously been near the place. He declined, however, either to explain his untruthful first statement, or give any other account of his mysterious absence.

One week ago Tademus had left the bungalow, carrying nothing but a light cane, and wearing a white flannel suit, canvas shoes, and a Panama. That was his idea of a tramping costume. He had returned, dressed in the same suit, hat and shoes. Moreover, though white, they looked neat as when he started, save for a few grass stains and the road's inevitable yellow clay about his shoe-soles.

If he had spent the week vagrant-wise, he had been remarkably successful in keeping his clothes clean.

"Asheville," thought the doctor. "He went by train, stopped at a hotel, and has returned without the faintest memory of his real doings. Lame, overtaxed nerves can play that sort of trick with a man's brain."

But he kept the opinion to himself. Like a good doctor, he soon dropped the whole subject, particularly because he saw that Tademus was deeply distressed and trying to conceal the fact.

On plea of taking a long-delayed vacation of his own, Locke remained some time at the bungalow, guarded his friend from the curiosity of those who had combed the hills for him, and did all in his power to restore him to health and a clear brain.

He was so far successful that Tademus returned to his classes in the fall, with Locke's consent.

To his classes—and death.

Wharton had known all this. He knew that Tademus' whereabouts during that mysterious week had never been learned. But the diary in the red book purported to cover the summer, including that week.

To Wharton, the record seemed so supremely curious that he took a liberty with what was now the university's property. He carried the book to Dr. Locke.

It was evening, and the latter was about to retire after a day's work that began before dawn.

"Personal, you say?" Locke handled the book, frowning slightly.

"Personal. But I feel—when you've finished reading that. I have a rather queer thing to tell you in addition. You can't understand till you've read it. I am almost sure that what is described here has a secret bearing on Professor Tademus' death."

"His heart failed. Overwork. There was no mystery in that."

"Maybe not, doctor. And yet—won't you please read?"

"Run through it aloud for me," said the doctor. "I couldn't read one of my own prescriptions tonight, and you are more familiar with that microscopic writing of his."

Wharton complied.

Monday, July 3.

Arrived yesterday. Not worse than expected, but bad enough. If Locke were here, he should be satisfied. I have absolutely no occupation. Walked and climbed for two hours, as prescribed. Spent the rest of day pacing up and down indoors. Enough walking, at least. I can't sit idle. I can't stop thinking. Locke is a fool!

Thursday, July 6.

Telegraphed Wharton today. He will express me the Swift binocular, some slides, cover-glasses, and a very little other apparatus. Locke is a fool! I shall follow his advice, but within reason. There is a room here lighted by five windows. Old Jake has cleared the bedroom furniture out. It has qualities as a laboratory. Not, of course, that I intend doing any real work. An hour or so a day of micrological observation will only make "resting" tolerable.

Tuesday, July 11.

Jake hitched up his "ol' gray mule" and has brought my three cases from the station' I unpacked the old Stephenson-Swift and set it up. The mere touch of it brought tears to my eyes. Locke's "rest-cure" has done that to my nerves!

After unpacking, though, I resolutely let the microscope and other things be. Walked ten miles up-hill and down. Tried to admire the landscape, as Locke advised, but can't see much in it. Rocks, trees, lumpy hills, yellow roads, sky, clouds, buzzards. Beauty! What beauty is there in this vast, clumsy world that is the outer husk for nature's real and delicate triumphs?

I saw a man painting today. He was swabbing at a canvas with huge, clumsy brushes. He had his easel set up by the road, and I stopped to see what any human being could find hereabout worth picturing.

And what had this painter, this artist, this lover of beauty chosen for a subject? Why, about a mile from here there is a clump of ugly, dark trees. A stream runs between them and the road. It is yellow with clay, and too swift. The more interesting microorganisms could not exist in it. A ram-shackle, plank bridge crosses it, leading to the grove, and there, between the trees, stand and lean some dreary, half-ruined huts.

That scene was the one which my "artist" had chosen for his subject.

For sheer curiosity I got into conversation with the fellow.

Unusual gibberish of chiaroscuro, flat tones, masses, et cetera. Not a definite thought in his head as to why he wished to paint those shacks. I learned one thing, though. He wasn't the isolated specimen of his kind I had thought him. Locke failed to tell me about Carcassonne. Think of it! Nearly a hundred of these insane pursuers of "beauty" are spending the summer within walking distance of the house I have promised to live in!

And the one who was painting the grove actually invited me to call on him! I smiled noncommittally, and came home. On the way I passed the branch road that leads to the place. I had always avoided that road, but I didn't know why until today. Imagine it! Nearly a hundred. Some of them women, I suppose. No, I shall keep discreetly away from Carcassonne.

Saturday, July 15.

Jake informs me that a band of gypsies have settled themselves in the grove which my Carcassonnian acquaintance chose to paint. They are living in the ruined huts. Now I shall avoid that road, too. Talk of solitude! Why, the hills are fairly swarming with artists, gypsies, and Lord knows who else. One might as well try to rest in a beehive!

Found some interesting variations of the ciliara living in a near-by pond. Wonderful! Have recorded over a dozen specimens in which the macronucleus is unquestionably double. Not lobed, not pulverate, as in Oxytricha, but double! My summer has not, after all, been wasted.

Felt singularly slack and tired this morning, and realized that I have hardly been out of the house in three days. Shall certainly take a long tramp tomorrow.

Monday, July 17.

Absent-mindedness betrayed me today. I had a very unpleasant experience. Resolutely keeping my promise to Locke, I sallied forth this afternoon and walked briskly for some distance. I had, however, forgotten the gypsies and took my old route.

Soon I met a woman, or rather a girl. She was arrayed in the tattered, brilliantly colored garments which women of these wandering tribes affect. There was a scarf about her head. I noticed because its blue was exactly the same brilliant hue of the sky over the mountains behind her. There was a stripe of yellow in it, too, and thrust in her sash she carried a great bunch of yellow flowers—wild honeysuckle, I think.

Her face was not dark, like the swart faces of most gypsies. On the contrary, the skin of it had a smooth, firm whiteness. Her features were fine and delicate.

Passing, we looked at one another, and I saw her eyes brighten in the strangest, most beautiful manner. I am sure that there was nothing bold or immodest in her glance. It was rather like the look of a person who recognizes an old acquaintance, and is glad of it. Yet we never met before. Had we met, I could not have forgotten her.

We passed without speaking, of course, and I walked on.

Meeting the girl, I had hardly thought of her as a gypsy, or indeed tried to classify her in any way. The impression she left was new in my experience. It was only on reaching the grove that I came to myself, as it were, and remembered Jake's story of the gypsies who are camping there.

Then I very quickly emerged from the vague, absurd happiness which sight of the girl had brought.

While talking with my Carcassonnian, I had observed that grove rather carefully. I had thought it perfect—that nothing added could increase the somber ugliness of its trees, nor the desolation of its gray, ruined, tumbledown old huts.

Today I learned better. To be perfect, ugliness must include sordid humanity.

The shacks, dreary in themselves, were hideous now. In their doorways lounged fat, unclean women nursing their filthy offspring. Older children, clothed in rags, caked with dirt, sprawled and fought among themselves. Their voices were the snarls of animals.

I realized that the girl with the sky-like scarf had come from here—out of this filth unspeakable!

A yellow cur, the mere, starved skeleton of a dog, came tearing down to the bridge. A rusty, jangling bell was tied about its neck with a string. The beast stopped on the far side and crouched there, yapping. Its anger seemed to surpass mere canine savagery. The lean jaws fairly writhed in maniacal but loathsomely feeble ferocity.

A few men, whiskered, dirty-faced, were gathered about a sort of forge erected in the grove. They were making something, beating it with hammers in the midst of showers of sparks. As the dog yapped, one of the men turned and saw me. He spoke to his mates, and to my dismay they stopped work and transferred their attention to me.

I was afraid that they would cross the bridge, and the idea of having to talk to them was for some reason inexpressibly revolting.

They stayed where they were, but one of them suddenly laughed out loudly, and held up to my view the thing upon which they had been hammering.

It was a great, clumsy, rough, iron trap. Even at that distance I could see the huge, jagged teeth, fit to maim a bear—or a man. It was the ugliest instrument I have ever seen.

I turned away and began walking toward home, and when I looked back they were at work again.

The sun shone brightly, but about the grove there seemed to be a queer darkness. It was like a place alone and aloof from the world. The trees, even, were different from the other mountain trees. Their heavy branches did not stir at all in the wind. They had a strange, dark, flat look against the sky, as though they had been cut from dark paper, or rather like the flat trees woven in a tapestry. That was it. The whole scene was like a flat, dark, unreal picture in tapestry.

I came straight home. My nerves are undoubtedly in bad shape, and I think I shall write Locke and ask him to prescribe medicine that will straighten me up. So far, his "rest-cure" has not been notably successful.

Wednesday, July 19.

I have met her again.

Last night I could not sleep at all. Round midnight I ceased trying, rose, dressed, and spent the rest of the night with the good old Stephenson-Swift. My light for night-work—a common oil lamp—is not very brilliant. This morning I suffered considerable pain behind the eyes, and determined to give Locke's "walking and open air" treatment another trial, though discouraged by previous results.

This time I remembered to turn my back on the road which leads to that hideous grove. The sunlight seemed to increase the pain I was already suffering. The air was hot, full of dust, and I had to walk slowly. At the slightest increase of pace my heart would set up a kind of fluttering, very unpleasant and giving me a sense of suffocation.

Then I came to the girl.

She was seated on a rock, her lap heaped with wild honeysuckle, and she was weaving the flower stems together.

Seeing me, she smiled.

"I have your garland finished," she said, "and mine soon will be."

One would have thought the rock a trysting place at which we had for a long time been accustomed to meet! In her hand she was extending to me a wreath, made of the honeysuckle flowers.

I can't imagine what made me act as I did. Weariness and the pain behind my eyes may have robbed me of my usual good sense.

Anyway, rather to my own surprise, I took her absurd wreath and sat down where she made room for me on the boulder.

After that we talked.

At this moment, only a few hours later, I couldn't say whether or not the girl's English was correct, nor exactly what she said. But I can remember the very sound of her voice.

I recall, too, that she told me her name Elva, and that when I asked for the rest of it, she informed me that one good name was enough for one good person.

That struck me as a charmingly humorous sally. I laughed like a boy—or a fool, God knows which!

Soon she had finished her second garland, and laughingly insisted that we each crown the other with flowers.

Imagine it. Had one of my students come by then, I am sure he would have been greatly startled. Professor Theron Tademus, seated on a rock with a gypsy girl, crowned with wild honeysuckle and adjusting a similar wreath to the girl's blue-scarfed head!

Luckily, neither the student nor anyone else passed, and in a few minutes she said something that brought me to my senses. Due to that inexplicable dimness of memory, I quote the sense, not her words.

"My father is a ruler among our people. You must visit us. For my sake, the people and my father will make you welcome."

She spoke with the gracious air of a princess, but I rose hastily from beside her. A vision of the grove had returned—dark, oppressive—like an old, dark tapestry, woven with the ugly forms and foliage. I remembered the horrible, filthy tribe from which this girl had sprung.

Without a word of farewell, I left her there on the rock. I did not look back, nor did she call after me. Not until reaching home, when I met old Jake at the door and saw him stare, did I remember the honeysuckle wreath. I was still wearing it, and carrying my hat.

Snatching at the flowers, I flung them in the ditch and retreated with what dignity I might into the bungalow's seclusion.

It is night now, and, a little while since, I went out again. The wreath is here in the room with me. The flowers were unsoiled by the ditch, and seem fresh as when she gave them to me. They are more fragrant than I had thought even wild honeysuckle could be.

Elva. Elva of the sky-blue scarf and the yellow honeysuckle

My eyes are heavy, but the pain behind them is gone. I think I shall sleep tonight.

Friday, July 21.

Is there any man so gullible as he who prides himself on his accuracy of observation?

I ask this in humility, for I am that man.

Yesterday I rose, feeling fresher than for weeks past. After all, Locke's treatment seemed worthy of respect. With that in mind, I put in only a few hours staining some of my binucleate cilia and finishing the slides.

All the last part of the afternoon I faithfully tramped the roads. There is undoubtedly a sort of broad, coarse charm in mere landscape, with its reaches of green, its distant purples, and the sky like a blue scarf flung over it all. Had the pain of my eyes not returned, I could almost have enjoyed those vistas.

Having walked farther than usual, it was deep dusk when I reached home. As if from ambush, a little figure dashed out from behind some rhododendrons. It seemed to be a child, a boy, though I couldn't see him clearly, nor how he was dressed.

He thrust something into my hand. To my astonishment, the thing was a spray of wild honeysuckle.

"Elva—Elva—Elva!"

The strange youngster was fairly dancing up and down before me, repeating the girl's name and nothing else.

Recovering myself, I surmised that Elva must have sent this boy, and sure enough, at my insistence he managed to stop prancing long enough to deliver her message.

Elva's grandmother, he said, was very ill. She had been ailing for days, but tonight the sickness was worse—much worse. Elva feared that her grandmother would die, and, "of course," the boy said, "no doctor will come for our sending!" She had remembered me, as the only friend she knew among the "outside people." Wouldn't I come and look at her poor, sick grandmother? And if I had any of the outside people's medicine in my house, would I please bring that with me?

Well, yes, I did hesitate. Aside from practical and obvious suspicions, I was possessed with a senseless horror for not only the gypsy tribe, but the grove itself.

But there was the spray of honeysuckle. In her need, she had sent that for a token—and sent it to me! Elva, of the sky-like scarf and laughing mouth.

"Wait here," I said to the boy, rather brusquely, and entered the house. I had remembered a pocket-case of simple remedies, none of which I had ever used, but there was a direction pamphlet with them. If I must play amateur physician, that might help. I looked for Jake, meaning to inform him of my proposed expedition. Though he had left a chicken broiling on the kitchen range, he was not about. He might have gone to the spring for water.

Passing out again, I called the boy, but received no answer. It was very dark. Toward sunset, the sky had clouded over, so that now I had not even the benefit of starlight.

I was angry with the boy for not waiting, but the road was familiar enough, even in the dark. At least, I thought it was, till, colliding with a clump of holly. I realized that I must have strayed off and across a bare stretch of yellow clay which defaces the Mountainside above Locke's bungalow.

I looked back for the guiding lights of its windows, but the trees hid them. However, the road couldn't be far off. After some stumbling about, I was sure that my feet were in the right track again. Somewhat later I perceived a faint, ruddy point of light, to the left and ahead of me.

As I walked toward it, the rapid rush and gurgle of water soon apprized me that I had reached the stream with the plank bridge across it.

There I stood for several minutes, staring toward the ruddy light. That was all I could see. It seemed, somehow, to cast no illumination about it.

There came a scamper of paws, the tinkle of a bell, and then a wild yapping broke out on the stream's far side. That vile, yellow cur, I thought. Elva, having imposed on my kindness to the extent of sending for me, might at least have arranged a better welcome than this.

When I pictured her, crouched in her bright, summer-colored garments, tending the dreadful old hag that her grandmother must be. The rest of the tribe were probably indifferent. She could not desert her sick—and there stood I, hesitant as any other coward!

For the dog's sake I took a firm grip on my cane. Feeling about with it, I found the bridge and crossed over.

Instantly something flung itself against my legs and was gone before I could hit out. I heard the dog leaping and barking all around me. It suddenly struck me that the beast's voice was not like that of the yellow cur. There was nothing savage in it. This was the cheerful, excited bark of a well-bred dog that welcomes its master, or its master's friend. And the bell that tinkled to every leap had a sweet, silvery note, different from the cracked jangle of the cur's bell.

I had hated and loathed that yellow brute, and to think that I need not combat the creature was a relief. The huts, as I recalled them, weren't fifty yards beyond the stream. There was no sign of a campfire. Just that one ruddy point of light.

I advanced—

Wharton paused suddenly in his reading. "Here," he interpolated, "begins that part of the diary which passed from commonplace to amazing. And the queer part is that in writing it, Professor Tademus seems to have been unaware that he was describing anything but an unusually pleasant experience."

Dr, Locke's heavy brows knit in a frown. "Pleasant!" he snapped. "The date of that entry?"

"July twenty-one."

"The day he disappeared. I see. Pleasant! And that gypsy girl—faugh! What an adventure for such a man! No wonder he tried to lie out of it. I don't think I care to hear the rest, Wharton. Whatever it is, my friend is dead. Let him rest."

"Oh, but wait," cried the young man, with startled earnestness. "Good Lord, doctor, do you believe I would bring this book even to you if it contained that kind of story—about Professor Tademus? No. Its amazing quality is along different lines than you can possibly suspect."

"Get on, then," grumbled Locke, and Wharton continued.

Suddenly, as though at a signal, not one, but a myriad of lights blazed into existence.

It was like walking out of a dark closet into broad day. The first dazzlement passing, I perceived that instead of the somber grove and ruined huts, I was facing a group of very beautiful houses.

It is curious how a previous and false assumption—will rule a man. Having believed myself at the gypsy encampment, several minutes passed before I could overcome my bewilderment and realize that after losing my road I had not actually regained it.

That I had somehow wandered into the other branch road, and reached, not the grove, but Carcassonne!

I had no idea, either, that this artists' colony could be such a really beautiful place. It is cut by no streets. The houses are set here and there over the surface of such green lawns as I have never seen in these mountains of rock and yellow clay.

(Dr. Locke started slightly in his chair. Carcassonne, as he had himself seen it, flashed before his memory. He did not interrupt, but from that moment his attention was alertly set, like a man who listens for the key word of a riddle.)

Everywhere were lights, hung in the flowering branches of trees, glowing upward from the grass, blazing from every door and window. Why they should have been turned on so abruptly, after that first darkness, I do not yet know.

Out of the nearest house a girl came walking. She was dressed charmingly, in thin, bright-colored silks. A bunch of wild honeysuckle was thrust in the girdle, and over her hair was flung a scarf of sky-like blue. I knew her instantly, and began to see a glimmering of the joke that had been played on me.

The dog bounded toward the girl. He was a magnificent collie. A tiny silver bell was attached to his neck by a broad ribbon.

I take credit for considerable aplomb in my immediate behavior. The girl had stopped a little way off. She was laughing, but I had certainly allowed myself to be victimized.

On my accusation, she at once admitted to having deceived me. She explained that, perceiving me to be misled by her appearance into thinking her one of the gypsies, she could not resist carrying out the joke. She had sent her small brother with the token and message.

I replied that the boy deserted me, and that I had nearly invaded the camp of real gypsies while looking for her and the fictitious dying grandmother.

At this she appeared even more greatly amused. Elva's mirth has a peculiarly contagious quality. Instead of being angry, I found myself laughing with her.

By this time quite a throng of people had emerged on the lawns, and leading me to a dignified, fine-looking old man who she said was her father, she presented me. In the moment, I hardly noticed that she used my first name only, Theron, which I had told her when we sat on the roadside boulder. I have observed since that all these people use the single name only, in presentation and intercourse. Though lacking personal experience with artists, I have heard that they are inclined to peculiar "fads" of unconventionality. I had never, however, imagined that they could be attractive to a man like myself, or pleasant to know.

I am enlightened. These Carcassonnian "colonists" are the only charming, altogether delightful people whom I have ever met.

One and all, they seemed acquainted with Elva's amusing jest at my expense. They laughed with us, but in recompense have made me one of themselves in the pleasantest manner.

I dined in the house of Elva's father. The dining-room, or rather hall, is a wonderful place. Due to much microscopic work, I am inclined to see only clumsiness—largeness—in what other people characterize as beauty. Carcassonne is different. There is a minute perfection about the architecture of these artists' houses, the texture of their clothes, and even the delicate contour of their faces, which I find amazingly agreeable.

There is no conventionality of costume among them. Both men and women dress as they please. Their individual taste is exquisite, and the result is an array of soft fabrics, and bright colors, flowerlike, rather than garish.

Till last night I never learned the charm of what is called "fancy dress," nor the genial effect it may exert on even a rather somber nature, such as I admit mine to be.

Elva, full of good-natured mischief, insisted that I must "dress for dinner." Her demand was instantly backed by the whole laughing throng. Carried off my feet in a way to which I am not at all used, I let them drape me in white robes, laced with silver embroideries like the delicate crystallization of hoar-frost. Dragged hilariously before a mirror, I was amazed at the change in my appearance.

Unlike the black, scarlet-hooded gown of my university, these glittering robes lent me not dignity, but a kind of—I can only call it a noble youthfulness. I looked younger, and at the same time keener—more alive. And either the contagious spirit of my companions, or some resurgence of boyishness filled me with a sudden desire to please; to be merry with the merry-makers, and—I must be frank—particularly to keep Elva's attention where it seemed temporarily fixed—on myself.

My success was unexpectedly brilliant. There is something in the very atmosphere of Carcassonne which, once yielded to, exhilarates like wine. I have never danced, nor desired to learn. Last night, after a banquet so perfect that I hardly recall its details, I danced. I danced with Elva—and with Elva—and always with Elva. She laughed aside all other partners. We danced on no polished floors, but out on the green lawns, under white, laughing stars. Our music was not orchestral. Wherever the light-footed couples chose to circle, there followed a young flutist, piping on his flute of white ivory.

Fluttering wings, driving clouds, wind tossed leaves—all the light, swift things of the air were in that music. It lifted and carried one with it. One did not need to learn. One danced! It seems, as I write, that the flute's piping is still in my ears, and that its echoes will never cease. Elva's voice is like the ivory flutels. Last night I was mad with the music and her voice. We danced—I know not how long, nor when we ceased.

This morning I awakened in a gold-and-ivory room, with round windows that were full of blue sky and crossed by blossoming branches. Dimly I recalled that Elva's father had urged me to accept his hospitality for the night.

Too much of such new happiness may have gone to my head, I'm afraid. At least, it was nothing stronger. At dinner I drank only one glass of wine-sparkling, golden stuff, but mild and with a taste like the fragrance of Elva's wild honeysuckle blooms.

It is midmorning now, and I am writing this seated on a marble bench beside a pool in the central court of my host's house. I am waiting for Elva, who excused herself to attend to some duty or other. I found this book in my pocket, and thought best to make an immediate record of not only a good joke on myself, but the only really pleasant social experience I have ever enjoyed.

I must lay aside these fanciful white robes, bid Elva good-by, and return to my lonely bungalow and Jake. The poor old man is probably tearing his hair over my unexplained absence. But I hope for another invitation to Carcassonne!

Saturday, July 22.

I seem to be "staying on" indefinitely. This won't do. I spoke to Elva of my extended visit, and she laughingly informed me that people who have drunk the wine and worn the woven robes of Carcassonne seldom wish to leave. She suggested that I give up trying to "escape" and spend my life here. Jest, of course; but I half wished her words were earnest. She and her people are spoiling me for the common, workaday world.

Not that they are idle, but their occupations as well as pleasures are of a delicate, fascinating beauty.

Whole families are stopping here, including the children. I don't care for children, as a rule, but these are harmless as butterflies. I met Elva's messenger, her brother. He is a funny, dear little elf. How even in the dark I fancied him one of those gypsy brats is hard to conceive. But then I took Elva herself for a gypsy!

My new friends engage in many pursuits besides painting. "Crafts," I believe they are called. This morning Elva took me around the shops—shops like architectural blossoms, carved out of the finest marble.

They make jewelry, weave fabrics, tool leather, and follow many other interesting occupations. Set in the midst of the lawns is a forge. Every part of it, even to the iron anvil, is embellished with a fernlike inlay of other metals. Several amateur silversmiths were at work there, but Elva hurried me away before I could see what they were about.

I have inquired for the young painter who first told me of Carcassonne and invited me to visit him there. I can't recall his name, but on describing him to Elva she replied vaguely that not every "outsider" was permanently welcome among her people.

I didn't press the question. Remembering the ugliness which that same painter had been committing to canvas, I could understand that his welcome among these exquisite workers might be short-lived. He was probably banished, or banished himself, soon after our interview on the road.

I must be careful, lest I wear out my own welcome. Yet the very thought of that old, rough, husk of a world that I must return to, brings back the sickness, and the pain behind my eyes that I had almost forgotten.

Sunday, July 23.

Elva! Her presence alone is delight. The sky is not bluer than her scarf and eyes. Sunlight is a duller gold than the wild honeysuckle she weaves in garlands for our heads.

Today, like child sweethearts, we carved our names on the smooth trunk of a tree. "Elva—Theron." And a wreath to shut them in. I am happy. Why—why, indeed should I leave Carcassonne?

Monday, July 24.

Still here, but this is the last night that I shall impose upon these regally hospitable people. An incident occurred today, pathetic from one viewpoint, outrageous from another. I was asleep when it happened, and only woke up at the sound of the gunshot.

Some rough young mountaineers rode into Carcassonne and wantonly killed Elva's collie dog. They claimed, I believe, that the unlucky animal attacked one of their number. A lie! The dog was gentle as a kitten. He probably leaped and barked around their horses and annoyed the young brutes. They had ridden off before I reached the scene.

Elva was crying, and no wonder. They had blown her pet's head clean off with a shotgun. Don't know what will be done about it. I wanted to go straight to the county sheriff, but Elva wouldn't have that. I pretended to give in but if her father doesn't see to the punishment of those men, I will. Murderous devils! Elva is too forgiving.

Wednesday, July 26.

I watched the silversmiths today. Elva was not with me. I had no idea that silver was worked like iron. They must use some peculiar amalgam, or it would melt in the furnace, instead of emerging white-hot, to be beaten with tiny, delicate hammers.

They were making a strange looking contraption. It was all silver, beaten into floral patterns, but the general shape was a riddle to me. Finally I asked one of the smiths what they were about. He is a tall fellow, with a merry, dark face.

"Guess!" he demanded.

"Can't. To my ignorance, it resembles a Chinese puzzle.'

"Something more curious than that."

"What?"

"An—elf-trap!" He laughed mischievously.

"Please!"

"Well, it's a trap anyway. See this?" The others had stepped back good-naturedly. With his hammer he pressed on a lever. Instantly two slender, jaw-like parts of the queer machine opened wide. They were set with needlelike points, or teeth. It was all red-hot, and when he removed his hammer the jaws clashed in a shower of sparks.

"It's a trap, of course." I was still puzzled.

"Yes, and a very remarkable one. This trap will not only catch, but it will recatch."

"I don't understand."

"If any creature, man, say—" he was laughing again-"walks into this trap, he may escape it. But sooner or later—soon, I should think—it will catch him again. That is why we call it an elf-trap!"

I perceived suddenly that he was making pure game of me. His mates were all laughing at the nonsense. I moved off, not offended, but perturbed in another way.

He and his absurd silver trap-toy had reminded me of the gypsies. What a horrible, rough iron thing that was which they had held up to me from their forge. Men capable of creating such an uncouthly cruel instrument as that jag toothed trap would be terrible to meet in the night. And I had come near blundering in among them—at night!

This won't do. I have been happy. Don't let me drop back into the morbidly nervous condition which invested those gypsies with more than human horror. Elva is calling me. I have been too long alone.

Friday, July 28.

Home again. I am writing this in my bungalow-laboratory. Gray dawn is breaking, and I have been at work here since midnight. Feel strangely depressed. Need breakfast, probably.

Last night Elva and I were together in the court of her father's house. The pool in the center of it is lighted from below to a golden glow. We were watching the goldfish, with their wide, filmy tails of living lace.

Suddenly I gave a sharp cry. I had seen a thing in the water more important than goldfish. Snatching out the small collecting bottle, without which I never go abroad, I made a quick pass at the pool's glowing surface.

Elva had started back, rather frightened.

"What is it?"

I held the bottle up and peered closely. There was no mistake.

"Dysteria," I said triumphantly. "Dysteria ciliata. Dysterlus giganticus, to give a unique specimen the separate name he deserves. Why, Elva, this enormous creature will give me a new insight on his entire species!"

"What enormous creature?"

For the first time I saw Elva nearly petulant. But I was filled with enthusiasm. I let her look in the bottle.

"There!" I ejaculated. "See him?"

"Where? I can't see anything but water—and a tiny speck in it."

"That," I explained proudly, "is dysterius giganticus. Large enough to be seen by the naked eye. Why, child, he's a monster of his kind. A fresh-water variety, too!"

I thrust the bottle in my pocket.

"Where are you going?"

"Home, of course. I can't get this fellow under the microscope any too quickly."

I had forgotten how wide apart are the scientific and artistic temperaments. No explanation I could make would persuade Elva that my remarkable capture was worth walking a mile to examine properly.

"You are all alike!" she cried. "All! You talk of love, but your love is for gold, or freedom, or some pitiful foolish nothingness like that speck of life you call by a long name—and leave me for!"

"But," I protested, "only for a little while. I shall come back."

She shook her head. This was Elva in a new mood, dark brows drawn, laughing mouth drooped to a sullen curve. I felt sorry to leave her angry, but my visit had already been preposterously long. Besides, a rush of desire had swept me to get back to my natural surroundings. I wanted the feel of the micrometer adjuster in my fingers, and to see the round, speckled white field under the lens pass from blurred chaos to perfect definition.

She let me go at last. I promised solemnly to come to her whenever she should send or call. Foolish child! Why, I can walk over to Carcassonne every day, if she likes.

I hear Jake rattling about in the breakfast-room. Conscience informs me that I have treated him rather badly. Wonder where he thought I was? Couldn't have been much worried, or he would have hunted me up in Carcassonne.

August 30.

I shall not make any further entries in this book. My day for the making of records is over, I think. Any sort of records. I go back to my classes next month. God knows what I shall say to them! Elva.

I may as well finish the story here.

Every day I find it harder to recall the details. If I hadn't this book, with what I wrote in it when I was— when I was there, I should believe that my brain had failed in earnest.

Locke said I couldn't have been in Carcassonne. He stood in the breakfast-room, with the sunlight striking across him. I saw him clearly. I saw the huge, coarse, ugly creature that he was. And in that minute, I knew.

But I wouldn't admit it, even to myself. I made him go with me to Carcassonne. There was no stream. There was no bridge.

The houses were wretched bungalows, set about on the bare, flat, yellow clay of the Mountainside. The people—artists, save the mark!—were a common, carelessly dressed, painting-aproned crowd who fulfilled my original idea of an artists colony.

Their coarse features and thick skins sickened me. Locke walked home beside me, very silent. I could hardly bear his company.

He was gross—coarse—human!

Toward evening, managing to escape his company, I stole up the road to the gypsy's grove. The huts were empty. That queer look, as of a flat, dark tapestry, was gone from the grove.

I crossed the plank bridge. Among the trees I found ashes, and a depression where the forge had stood. Something else, too. A dog, or rather its unburied remains. The yellow cur. Its head had been blown off by a shotgun. An ugly little bell lay in the mess, tied to a piece of string.

One of the trees—it had a smooth trunk—and carved in the bark—I can't write it. I went away and left those two names carved there.

The wild honeysuckle has almost ceased to bloom. I can leave now. Locke says I am well, and that I can return to my classes.

I have not entered my laboratory since that morning. Locke admires my "willpower" for dropping all that till physical health should have returned. Will-power! I shall never, as long as I live, look into a microscope again.

Perhaps she will know that somehow, and send or call for me quickly.

I have drunk the wine and worn the woven robes of her people. They made me one of them. Is it right that they should cast me out, because I did not understand what I have since guessed the meaning of so well?

I can't bear the human folk about me. They are clumsy, revolting. And I can't work.

God only knows what I shall say to my classes.

Here is the end of my last record—till she calls!

There was silence in Locke's private study. At last the doctor expelled his breath in a long sigh. He might have been holding it all the time.

"Great-Heavens!" he ejaculated. "Poor old Tademus! And I thought his trouble in the summer there was a temporary lapse. But he talked like a sane man. Acted like one, too, by Jove! With his mind in that condition! And in spite of the posse, he must have been with the gypsies all that week. You can see it. Even through his delusions, you catch occasional notes of reality.

"I heard of that dog-shooting, and he speaks of being asleep when it happened. Where was he concealed that the posse didn't find him? Drugged and hidden under some filthy heap of rags in one of the huts, do you think? And why hide him at all, and then let him go? He returned the very day they left."

At the volley of questions, Wharton shook his head.

"I can't even guess about that. He was certainly among the gypsies. But as for his delusions, to call them so, there is a kind of beauty and coherence about them which I—well, which I don't like!"

The doctor eyed him sharply.

"You can't mean that you-"

"Doctor," said Wharton softly, "do you recall what he wrote of the silversmiths and their work? They were making an elf-trap. Well, I think the elf-trap—caught him!"

"What?"

Locke's tired eyes opened wide. A look of alarm flashed into them. The alarm was for Wharton, not himself.

"Wait!" said the latter. "I haven't finished. You know that I was in the classroom at the moment when Professor Tademus died?"

"Yes?"

"Yes! I was the first to reach him. But before that, I stood near the desk. There are three windows at the foot of that room. Every other man there faced the desk. I faced the windows. The professor entered, laid down his book and turned to the class. As he did so, a head appeared in one of those windows. They are close to the ground, and a person standing outside could easily look in.

"The head was a woman's. No, I am not inventing this. I saw her head, draped in a blue scarf. I noticed, because the scarf's blueness gave me the strangest thrill of delight. It was the exact blue of the sky behind it. Then she had raised her hand. I saw it. In her fingers was a spray of yellow flowers—yellow as sunshine. She waved them in a beckoning motion. Like this.

"Then Tademus dropped.

"And there are legends, you know, of strange people, either more or less than human, who appear as gypsies, but are not the real gypsies, that possess queer powers. Their outer appearance is rough and vile, but behind that, as a veil, they live a wonderful hidden life of their own.

"And a man who has been with them once is caught—caught in the real elf-trap, which the smiths' work only symbolized. He may escape, but he can't forget nor be joined again with his own race, while to return among them, he must walk the dark road that Tademus had taken when she called.

"Oh. I've scoffed at 'old wives' tales' with the rest of our overeducated, modern kind. I can't ever scoff again, you see, because-

"What's that? A prescription? For me? Why, doctor, you don't yet understand. I saw her, I tell you. Elva! Elva! Elva, of the wild honeysuckle and the sky-like scarf!"

Gertrude Barrows Bennett – A Short Biography

Gertrude Mabel Barrows was born in Minneapolis on 18th September 1884, to Charles, a Civil War veteran from Illinois, and Caroline Barrows (née Hatch).

Gertrude completed school up to the eighth grade, then switched to night school to study illustration. Although she had hopes of becoming an illustrator it was a goal she never achieved. As a fall back she began working as a stenographer, a career which she would keep to for the rest of her life.

But Gertrude had talent, writer's talent. Her first short story was written when she was just 17. Not you would think the usual subjects of curious teenage girls with headstrong ambitions but a science fiction story entitled 'The Curious Experience of Thomas Dunbar'. At the turn of the century magazines stands were full of cheap pulp magazines published weekly, fortnightly or monthly. She mailed the finished story to Argosy, then one of the top and most well known of the pulp magazines. The story was accepted and published in the March 1904 issue.

After this nothing seems to happen in her career as a writer for over a decade.

In 1909 Gertrude married the British journalist and explorer Stewart Bennett, and they moved to Philadelphia. A daughter was born the following year. Married life seemed blissful.

However tragedy now stepped in. Stewart died in a tropical storm while on a treasure hunting expedition.

Gertrude continued to work as a stenographer whilst trying to raise her new-born, and now fatherless, daughter.

Despite these pressures there is evidence that Gertrude began to write again. The obvious choice of interest continued to be ignored in favour of science fiction and with it a focus on dark fantasy.

Her mother, Caroline was an invalid and when Gertrude's father died she now also took on the care of her Mother.

During this time period Gertrude began to write a number of short stories, and then novels, in order to support her family. It was certainly the most productive part of her writing career.

Once Gertrude began to take care of her mother, she decided to return to fiction writing as a means of supporting her family. The first story she completed after her return to writing was the novella 'The Nightmare,' which appeared in All-Story Weekly in 1917. The story is set on an island separated from the rest of the world, on which evolution has taken a different course.

In submitting the story for publication Gertrude had requested that if it was accepted to be published then to use her pseudonym of Jean Vail. The Editor kindly agreed but under the pseudonym of Francis Stevens.

All-Story Weekly readers were pleased with the story as was Gertrude with her new name. She now wrote only under the moniker 'Francis Stevens'.

Over the next few years, Gertrude was rather more prolific than she had been. And her ideas were excellent and seemed also to influence others. (Indeed following the 'Nightmare' a year later was the similarly themed The Land That Time Forgot by Edgar Rice Burroughs).

Her short story "Friend Island" (All-Story Weekly, 1918), for example, is set in a 22nd-century ruled by women. Another story is the novella 'Serapion' (Argosy, 1920), about a man possessed by a supernatural creature.

In 1918 she published her first, and probably her best work the novel' The Citadel of Fear' (printed in several parts by Argosy, 1918). This lost world story focuses on a long-forgotten Aztec city, which is "rediscovered" during World War I.

A year later she published her only science fiction novel, 'The Heads of Cerberus' (The Thrill Book, 1919). One of the first dystopian novels, the book features a "grey dust from a silver phial" which transports anyone who inhales it to a totalitarian Philadelphia of 2118 AD

One of Bennett's most famous novels was 'Claimed!' (Argosy, 1920), in which a supernatural artefact summons an ancient and powerful god to early 20th century New Jersey. At the time it was said to be "one of the strangest and most compelling science fantasy novels you will ever read".

Her publisher at the time, The Thrill Book, had accepted several more of her stories for publication in the coming months. Her career was looking very promising. Sadly The Thrill Book failed only seven months after its first issue. Whatever stories it had stockpiled were lost.

Her Mother died in 1920 and once again Gertrude put her pen to one side.

In the mid-1920s, she moved to California. And for Gertrude her career was over. It was originally believed that she died in 1939 and for some years was estranged from her daughter. However recent new research has provided a death certificate stating that Gertrude Barrows Bennett died on February 2nd, 1948 at the age of 63 in San Francisco, California.

She did leave behind one mystery. For several decades her pseudonym Francis Stevens was believed to be that of the very popular Abraham Merritt. It was only finally revealed to be hers with the1952 book publication of 'Citadel of Fear'. Why no-one had spoken earlier to reveal this is not known.

In the ensuing years her work was barely printed but at the turn of the century a new interest and appetite had been shown for her works. Some have said she is the mother of 'Dark Fantasy' and her works had an influence both on Merritt and the dark master himself H.P. Lovecraft.

Gertrude Barrows Bennett - A Concise Bibliography

The Citadel of Fear (1918)
The Labyrinth (All-Story Weekly, July 27, August 3, and August 10, 1918)
The Heads of Cerberus (Thrill Book, 15 August 1919)
Avalon (Argosy, August 16 to September 6, 1919)
Claimed (Argosy, 1920)

Short Stories and Novellas

The Curious Experience of Thomas Dunbar (Argosy, March, 1904; as by G. M. Barrows)
The Nightmare, (All-Story Weekly, April 14, 1917)
Friend Island (All-Story Weekly, September 7, 1918)
Behind the Curtain (All-Story Weekly, September 21, 1918)
Unseen—Unfeared (People's Favorite Magazine Feb. 10, 1919)
The Elf-Trap (Argosy, July 5, 1919)
Serapion (Argosy Weekly, June 19, June 26, and July 3, 1920)
Sunfire (Weird Tales, July–August 1923, and September 1923)

www.ingramcontent.com/pod-product-compliance
Lightning Source LLC
Chambersburg PA
CBHW061505170626
46811CB00004B/1615